ROSIE IS MY BEST FRIEND

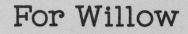

For Willow

SIMON & SCHUSTER

First published in Great Britain in 2019 by Simon & Schuster UK Ltd

1st Floor, 222 Gray's Inn Road, London, WC1X 8HB ▪ A CBS Company

Text and illustrations copyright © 2019 Ali Pye

The right of Ali Pye to be identified as the author and illustrator of this work has been

asserted by her in accordance with the Copyright, Designs and Patents Act, 1988

All rights reserved, including the right of reproduction in whole or in part in any form

A CIP catalogue record for this book is available from the British Library upon request

978-1-4711-7249-6 (HB) ▪ 978-1-4711-7250-2 (PB) ▪ 978-1-4711-7251-9 (eBook)

Printed in China ▪ 10 9 8 7 6 5 4 3 2 1

ROSIE IS MY BEST FRIEND

Ali Pye

SIMON & SCHUSTER

London   New York   Sydney   Toronto   New Delhi

Today has been **SUCH** a good day.

It's been **BRILLIANT!**

AMAZING!

That's because I spent it with Rosie.

You see, Rosie is my **Very Best Friend**.
And I think I'm hers.

The day was fun right from the moment we woke up.
Yes, it WAS a bit before everyone else did . . .

but Rosie and I made sure we were **VERY** quiet.

Well, that was the plan anyway.

Rosie is still young and has a lot to learn,
so after breakfast we practised her tricks.

"Sit."

"Fetch."

"Lie down."

She's doing really well.

Next, we helped with some jobs.
We helped in the garden . . .

and we helped do the shopping . . .

and then we helped tidy the house.

We would have helped some more, but the
grown-ups said we'd done enough for now.
They were really quite firm about it.

Instead, they said we should go
outside for a *good long walk*,
so we made a picnic and set off
for the park.

Rosie only has little legs,

but she can walk for miles.

We couldn't help getting slightly muddy on the way – but we don't mind a few spots of mud!

At the park, all our friends were zipping and zooming around madly, so we zipped and we zoomed with them, too.

I've got lots of friends, but there's just something special between Rosie and me.

Soon it was time to head home. We were walking along, singing our favourite song, when all of a sudden we saw a big, fierce dog.

It was MASSIVE,
the biggest dog I've ever seen!

Rosie was scared, I could tell, but I'm sure she felt braver having **ME** nearby.

I might have looked a bit scared too, but I was only pretending.

After tea, we went exploring! I'm happy anywhere as long as Rosie is next to me:

from the most faraway planet in outer space . . .

to the deepest depths of the ocean.

But when we've returned from our travels, this is our most favourite place of all.

What a day I've had with Rosie!
And do you know, I think tomorrow
could be even better.

I just can't wait to spend it together.

There's no one quite like Rosie:
she is gentle, and funny, and kind.

Yes, Rosie is the **Very Best Friend** . . . .

 . . . that a dog could ever have!

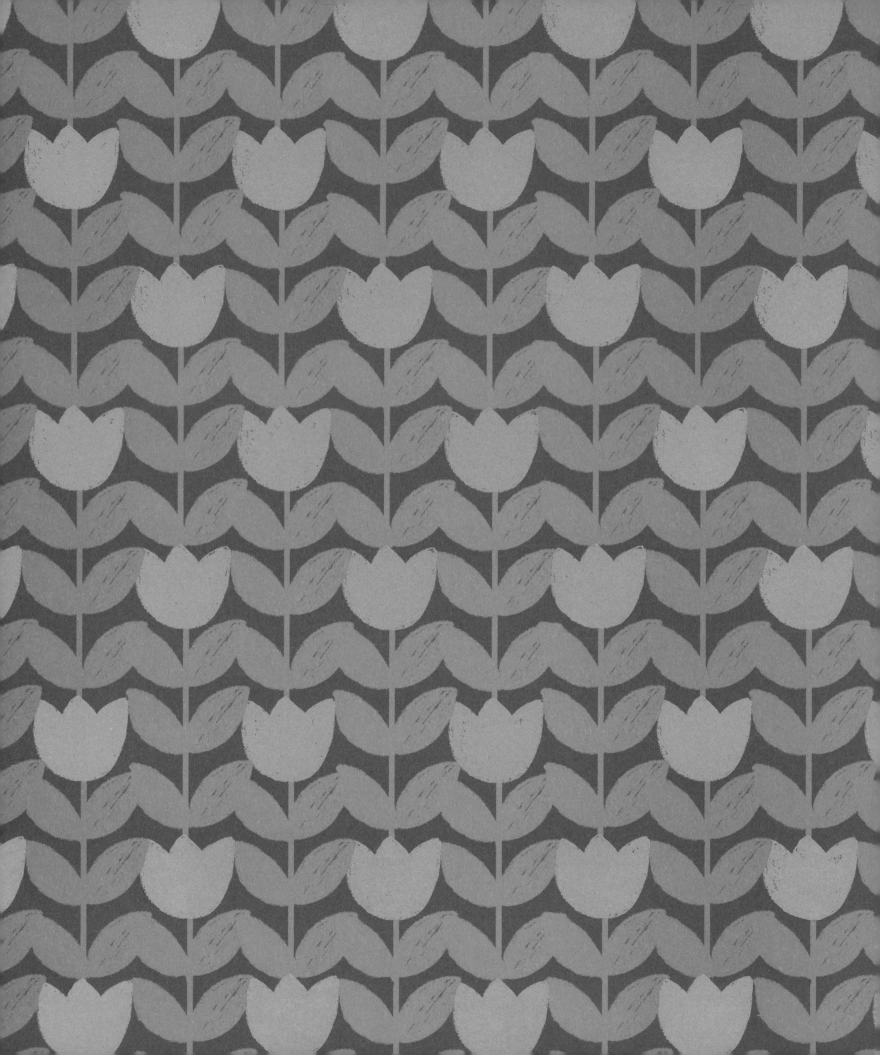